EVERYONE LOVES HORRID HENRY!

"All *Horrid Henry* stories are a joy to read"
DAILY MAIL

"Loved by primary school children the world over"
INDEPENDENT

"There is little like *Horrid Henry* to get young
boys, especially, off the reading blocks"
THE TIMES

"I love reading these books to my girls"
FRANK LAMPARD

"You can't go wrong with a *Horrid Henry* title if you have
children who are reluctant to read: his mischievous antics
hold universal appeal for boys and girls . . . So hilarious it
will have young readers laughing out loud. These easy-to-
read stories are a great way to develop reading skills"
WATERSTONES BOOKS QUARTERLY

"Henry speaks to the imp in every child. The humour is pitch
perfect and, of course, Francesca Simon absolutely nails
the dynamics of sibling rivalry"
BOOKSELLER

"Few naughty characters have captured the hearts
of children like *Horrid Henry*. The anarchic comedy of
Francesca Simon's writing coupled with Tony Ross's
scratchy illustrations make Henry one of the
most enduring menaces in literature"

D0620621

HORRID HENRY

SCHOOL STINKS

FRANCESCA SIMON

ILLUSTRATED BY TONY ROSS

Orion

ORION CHILDREN'S BOOKS

Stories originally published in "Horrid Henry: Tricking the Tooth Fairy", "Horrid Henry: Zombie Vampire", "Horrid Henry: Krazy Ketchup", "Horrid Henry: The Mummy's Curse", and "Horrid Henry: Up, Up and Away" respectively.

This collection first published in Great Britain in 2021 by Hodder and Stoughton

1 3 5 7 9 10 8 6 4 2

Text © Francesca Simon, 1996, 2011, 2014, 2000, 2019
Illustrations © Tony Ross, 1996, 2011, 2014, 2000, 2019
Puzzles and activities © Orion Children's Books, 2021

A CIP catalogue record for this book is available from the British Library.

ISBN 978 1 51010 877 6

Printed and bound in Great Britain by Clays Ltd, Elcograf S.p.A.

The paper and board used in this book are from well-managed forests and other
responsible sources.

MIX
Paper from
responsible sources
FSC® C104740
www.fsc.org

Orion Children's Books
An imprint of
Hachette Children's Group
Part of Hodder and Stoughton
Carmelite House
50 Victoria Embankment
London EC4Y 0DZ

An Hachette UK Company
www.hachette.co.uk

www.hachettechildrens.co.uk
www.horridhenry.co.uk

CONTENTS

MEET THE

200 CM

175 CM

150 CM
HENRY

125 CM
PETER

100 CM

75 CM

50 CM

25 CM

0 CM

HORRID HENRY'S

NEW TEACHER

"Now Henry," said Dad. "Today is the first day of school. A chance for a fresh start with a new teacher."

"Yeah, yeah," scowled Horrid Henry.

He hated the first day of term. Another year, another teacher to show who was **BOSS**. His first teacher, Miss Marvel, had run *screaming* from the classroom after *two* weeks. His next teacher, Mrs Zip, had run *screaming* from the classroom after **ONE** day. Breaking in new teachers wasn't easy, thought

Henry, but someone had to do it.

Dad got out a piece of paper and waved it.

"Henry, I never want to read another school report like this again," he said. "Why can't your school reports be like Peter's?"

Henry started whistling.

"Pay attention, Henry," shouted Dad. "This is important. Look at this report."

HENRY'S SCHOOL REPORT

It has been horrible Teaching Henry this year. He is rude, lazy and disruptive. The worst student I have ever taught.

Behaviour: Horrid

English: Horrid

Maths: Horrid

Science: Horrid

P.E: Horrid

"What about *my* report?" said
Perfect Peter.

Dad *beamed*.

"Your report was perfect, Peter,"
said Dad. "Keep up the wonderful
work."

Peter smiled proudly.

PETER'S SCHOOL REPORT

It has been a pleasure
teaching Peter this year. He is
polite, hard-working and
co-operative. The best student I
have ever taught.

Behaviour: Perfect

English: Perfect

Maths: Perfect

Science: Perfect

P.E: Perfect

"You'll just have to try harder, Henry," said Peter, smirking.

Horrid Henry was a **SHARK** sinking his teeth into a drowning sailor.

"**OWWWW**," shrieked Peter. "Henry bit me!"

"Don't be **horrid**, Henry!" shouted Dad. "Or no TV for a week."

"I don't care," muttered Henry. When he became king he'd make it a law that PARENTS, not children, had to go to school.

Horrid Henry *PUSHED* and *shoved* his way into class and *grabbed* the seat next to Rude Ralph.

"**NAH NAH NE NAH NAH**, I've got a new football," said Ralph.

Henry didn't have a football. He'd **kicked** his through Moody Margaret's window.

"Who cares?" said Horrid Henry.

The classroom door **SLAMMED**. It was Mr Nerdon, the toughest, **MEANEST**, **NASTIEST** teacher in the school.

"**SILENCE!**" he said, glaring at them with his **bulging** eyes. "I don't

want to hear a sound. I don't even
want to hear anyone breathe."

The class held its breath.

"**GOOD**!" he growled. "I'm Mr Nerdon."

Henry **snorted**. What a stupid name.

"**Nerd**," he whispered to Ralph.

Rude Ralph GIGGLED.

"Nerdy Nerd," whispered Horrid
Henry, SNICKERING.

Mr Nerdon walked up to Henry and
jabbed his finger in his face.

"Quiet, you **HORRIBLE** boy!" said
Mr Nerdon. "I've got my eye on you.
Oh yes. I've heard about your other

teachers. Bah! I'm made of **STRONGER STUFF**. There will be **NO NONSENSE** in *my* class."

We'll see about that, thought Henry.

"Our first sums for the year are on the board. Now get to work," ordered Mr Nerdon.

Horrid Henry had an idea.

Quickly he **scribbled** a note to Ralph.

Ralph - I bet you that I can make Mr. Nerdon run screaming out of class by the end of lunchtime.

No way, Henry

If I do will you give me your new football?

O.K. But if you don't, you have to give me your pound coin.

O.K.

Horrid Henry took a deep breath and went to work. He rolled up some paper, stuffed it in his mouth, and **SPAT** it out.

The spitball *whizzed* through the air and **pinged** Mr Nerdon on the back of his neck.

Mr Nerdon wheeled round.

"**YOU!**" snapped Mr Nerdon. "**DON'T YOU MESS WITH ME!**"

"It wasn't *me!*" said Henry. "It was Ralph."

"**LIAR!**" said Mr Nerdon. "Sit at the back of the class."

Horrid Henry moved his seat next
to Clever Clare.

"Move over, Henry!" HISSED Clare.
"You're on my side of the desk."

Henry *shoved* her.

"Move over yourself," he HISSED back.

Then Horrid Henry reached over
and **BROKE** Clare's pencil.

"HENRY BROKE MY PENCIL!" shrieked Clare.

Mr Nerdon moved Henry next
to Weepy William.

Henry PINCHED him.

Mr Nerdon moved Henry next to
Tough Toby.

Henry **JIGGLED** the desk.

Mr Nerdon moved Henry next to Lazy Linda.

Henry **scribbled** all over her paper.

Mr Nerdon moved Henry next to Moody Margaret.

Moody Margaret drew a line down the middle of the desk.

"Cross that line, Henry, and you're **DEAD**," said Margaret under her breath.

Henry looked up. Mr Nerdon was writing spelling words on the board.

Henry started to rub out
Margaret's line.

"**STOP IT, HENRY**," said Mr Nerdon,
without turning round.

Henry stopped.

Mr Nerdon continued writing.

Henry *pulled* Margaret's hair.

Mr Nerdon moved Henry next to
Beefy Bert, the **BIGGEST** boy
in the class.

Beefy Bert was
chewing his pencil
and trying to
add 2 + 2

without much luck.

Horrid Henry inched his chair on to Beefy Bert's side of the desk.

Bert ignored him.

Henry poked him.

Bert ignored him.

Henry HIT him.

The next thing Henry knew he was lying on the floor, looking up at the ceiling. Beefy Bert continued **chewing** his pencil.

"What happened, Bert?" said Mr Nerdon.

"**I dunno**," said Beefy Bert.

"Get up off the floor, Henry!" said Mr Nerdon. A faint smile appeared on the teacher's slimy lips.

"He **HIT** me!" said Henry. He'd never felt such a punch in his life.

"It was an accident," said Mr Nerdon. He **smirked**. "You'll sit

next to Bert from now on."

That's it, thought Henry. Now it's **war**.

"How absurd, to be a nerdy bird," said Horrid Henry behind Mr Nerdon's back.

Slowly Mr Nerdon turned and walked towards him. His hand was **CLENCHED** into a fist.

"Since you're so good at rhyming," said Mr Nerdon, "everyone write a poem. Now."

Henry *slumped* in his seat and **GROANED**.

A poem! **YUCK!** He hated poems. Even the word *poem* made him want to throw up.

Horrid Henry caught Rude Ralph's eye. Ralph was GRINNING and mouthing, "A pound, a pound!" at him. Time was running out. Despite Henry's best efforts, Mr Nerdon still hadn't run **SCREAMING** from the class. Henry would have to act fast to get that football.

What **horrible** poem could he write?

Horrid Henry *smiled*. Quickly he

picked up his pencil and went to
work.

"Now, who's my first victim?" said Mr
Nerdon. He looked round the room.
"Susan! Read your poem."

Sour Susan stood up and read:

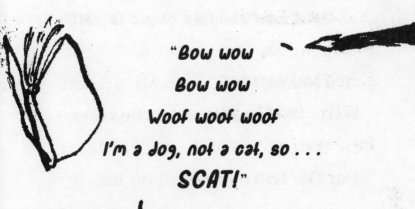

"Bow wow
Bow wow
Woof woof woof
I'm a dog, not a cat, so . . .
SCAT!"

"NOT ENOUGH RHYMES," said Mr Nerdon.

"Next . . ." He looked round the room.

"Graham!"

Greedy Graham stood up and read:

"Chocolate chocolate chocolate sweet,
Cakes and doughnuts can't be beat.
Ice cream is my favourite treat
With lots and lots of pie to eat!"

"TOO MANY RHYMES," said Mr Nerdon.

"Next . . ." He scowled at the class.

Henry tried to look as if he didn't
want the teacher to call on him.

28

"**HENRY!**" snapped Mr Nerdon.
"Read your poem.'"

Horrid Henry stood up and read:

"*Pirates puke on stormy seas,*
Giants spew on top of trees."

Henry peeked at Mr
Nerdon. He looked pale.
Henry continued to read:

"*Kings are sick in golden loos,*
Dogs throw up on Daddy's
shoes."

Henry peeked again at Mr Nerdon. He looked green. Any minute now, thought Henry, and he'll be out of here screaming. He read on:

"Babies love to make a MESS,
Down the front of Mum's best dress
And what car ride would be complete,
Without the STINK of last night's treat?"

"That's enough," choked Mr Nerdon.

"Wait, I haven't got to the good bit," said Horrid Henry.

"I said that's enough!" gasped

Mr Nerdon. "You fail."

He made a big **BLACK** mark in his book.

"I *threw up* on the boat!" shouted Greedy Graham.

"I *threw up* on the plane!" shouted Sour Susan.

"I *threw up* in the car!" shouted Dizzy Dave.

"I SAID THAT'S ENOUGH!"

ordered Mr Nerdon. He glared at Horrid Henry. "Get out of here, all of you! It's lunchtime."

RATS, thought Henry. Mr Nerdon was one tough teacher.

Rude Ralph grabbed him.

"**HA HA**, Henry," said Ralph. "You lose. Gimme that pound."

"No," said Henry. "I've got until the end of lunch."

"You can't do anything to him between now and then," said Ralph.

"Oh yeah?" said Henry. "Watch me."

Then Henry had a *wonderful*, *spectacular* idea. This was it. The best plan he'd ever had. Someday someone would stick a plaque on

the school wall celebrating Henry's
genius. There would be songs written
about him. He'd probably even get a
medal. But first things first. In order
for his plan to work to perfection, he
needed Peter.

Perfect Peter was playing hopscotch
with his friends Tidy Ted and
Spotless Sam.

"Hey Peter," said Henry. "How
would you like to be a real member of
the Purple Hand?"

The PURPLE HAND was Horrid Henry's
secret club. Peter had wanted to join

for ages, but naturally Henry would never let him.

Peter's jaw **DROPPED** open.

"Me?" said Peter.

"Yes," said Henry. "If you can pass the SECRET CLUB test."

"What do I have to do?" said Peter.

"It's *tricky*," said Henry. "And probably much too **HARD** for you."

"Tell me, tell me," said Peter.

"All you have to do is lie down right there below that window and stay absolutely still. You mustn't move until I tell you to."

"Why?" said Peter.

"Because **THAT'S** the test," said Henry.

Perfect Peter thought for a moment.

"Are you going to **DROP** something on me?"

"No," said Henry.

"OK," said Peter. He lay down obediently.

"And I need your shoes," said Henry.

"Why?" said Peter.

Henry **SCOWLED**.

"Do you want to be in the SECRET CLUB or not?" said Henry.

"I do," said Peter.

"Then give me your shoes and be quiet," said Henry. "I'll be checking on you. If I see you *moving* one LITTLE bit you can't be in my club."

Peter gave Henry his trainers, then lay still as a statue.

Horrid Henry *grabbed* the shoes, then DASHED up the stairs to his classroom.

It was empty. Good.

Horrid Henry went over to the

window and opened it. Then he stood there, holding one of Peter's shoes in each hand.

Henry waited until he heard Mr Nerdon's footsteps. Then he went into action.

"**HELP!**" shouted Horrid Henry.

"**HELP!**"

Mr Nerdon entered. He saw Henry and *glowered*.

"What are you doing here? Get out!"

"**HELP!**" shouted Henry. "I can't hold on to him much longer . . . he's *slipping* .

.. AAAHHH, HE'S FALLEN!"

Horrid Henry held up the empty shoes.

"He's gone," whispered Henry. He peeked out of the window. "Ugghh, I can't look."

Mr Nerdon went pale. He ran to the window and saw *Perfect Peter*

lying still and shoeless on the ground below.

"Oh no," gasped Mr Nerdon.

"I'm sorry," panted Henry. "I tried to hold on to him, honest, I—"

"**HELP!**" screamed Mr Nerdon. He raced down the stairs. "**POLICE! FIRE! AMBULANCE! HELP! HELP!**"

He ran over to Peter and knelt by his still body.

"Can I get up now, Henry?" said

Perfect Peter.

"What!?" gasped Mr Nerdon. "What did you say?"

Then the TERRIBLE truth dawned. He, Ninius Nerdon, had been *tricked*.

"YOU HORRID BOY! GO STRAIGHT TO THE HEAD TEACHER – NOW!" *screeched* Mr Nerdon.

Perfect Peter jumped to his feet. "But . . . but—" SPLUTTERED Perfect Peter

"NOW!" screamed Mr Nerdon. "How dare you! To the head!"

"AAAGGGHHHH," shrieked Peter.

He slunk off to the head's office,
weeping.

Mr Nerdon turned to race up the
stairs to grab Henry.

"**I'LL GET YOU, HENRY!**" he
SCREAMED. His face was white. He
looked as if he were going to faint.

"HELP," squeaked Mr Nerdon.

Then he fainted.

CLUNK! THUNK! THUD!

**NEE NAW NEE
NAW NEE NAW!**

When the ambulance arrived, the only person lying on the ground was Mr Nerdon. They *scooped* him on to a stretcher and took him away.

The *perfect* end to a *perfect* day, thought Horrid Henry, **throwing** his new football in the air. Peter sent home in disgrace. Mr Nerdon gone for good. Even the news that scary Miss Battle-Axe would be teaching Henry's class didn't bother him.

After all, tomorrow was another day.

HORRID
HENRY
AND THE
NUDIE FOODIE

"Children, I have some thrilling news," burbled Mrs Oddbod.

Horrid Henry groaned. His idea of **THRILLING** news and Mrs Oddbod's idea of **THRILLING** news were not the same. **THRILLING** news would be Mutant Max replacing Mrs Oddbod as Head. **THRILLING** news would be **MISS BATTLE-AXE** being whisked off to ancient Rome to be a gladiator. **THRILLING** news would be **MOODY MARGARET** dumped in a swamp and Perfect Peter sent to prison.

THRILLING news wasn't new coat hooks and who was in the *Good as Gold* book.

But wait. What was Mrs Oddbod saying?

"Our school has been chosen to be a healthy-eating school. Our new healthy and nutritious school meals will be an example for schools everywhere."

Horrid Henry sat up. What? Healthy eating? Oh no. Henry knew what grown-ups meant by healthy food. **CELERY**. *Beetroot*.

AUBERGINE TOWERS. Anything that tasted yucky and looked **REVOLTING** was bound to be good for him. Anything that tasted **YUMMY** was bound to be bad. Henry had plenty of healthy eating at home. Was nowhere safe?

"And guess who's going to help make our school a beacon of healthy eating?" babbled Mrs Oddbod. "Only the world-famous chef, **Mr Nudie Foodie.**"

Rude Ralph snorted. "Nudie," he jeered.

Mr Nudie Foodie? thought Horrid Henry. What kind of stupid name was that? Were there really parents out there whose surname was Foodie, who'd decided that the perfect name for their son was **Nudie?**

"And here he is, in person," proclaimed Mrs Oddbod.

The children clapped as a shaggy-haired man wearing a red-checked apron and a chef's hat **bounced** to the front of the auditorium.

"From today your school will be the place for delicious, nutritious food," he beamed. "I'm not **nude**, it's my food that's **nude!** My delicious, **YUMMALICIOUS** grub is just plain scrummy."

Horrid Henry couldn't believe his ears. Just plain, delicious food? Why,

that was exactly what Horrid Henry
loved. Plain burgers. Plain pizzas
just with cheese and nothing else.
No sneaky *flabby* pieces of aubergine
or **GRISLY** chunks of red pepper
ruining the topping. Plain chips
slathered in **ketchup**. No funny bits.
No strange green stuff. Three cheers
to **MORE BURGERS**, **MORE CHIPS** and **MORE
PIZZA!**

 Horrid Henry could see it now.
Obviously, he'd be asked to create
the **YUMMY** new school menu of
plain, delicious food.

MONDAY: CRISPS, CHIPS, ICE CREAM, CAKE, BURGERS

TUESDAY: BURGERS, CHIPS, CRISPS, CHOCOLATE

WEDNESDAY: PIZZA, CHIPS, CRISPS, ICE CREAM

THURSDAY: CHOCOLATE CAKE

FRIDAY: BURGERS, PIZZA, CHIPS, CRISPS, CAKE, ICE CREAM

(After all, it was the end of the week, and nice to celebrate.) Oh, and **FIZZYWIZZ** drinks every day, and **chocolate milk**. There! A lovely,

51

healthy, plain, nutritious and delicious menu that everyone would love. Because, let's face it, at the moment school dinners *were* **HORRID**. They only served burgers and chips once a week, thought Horrid Henry indignantly. Well, he'd soon sort *that* out.

In fact, maybe *he* should be a famous chef when he got older. *Chef Henry, the burger wizard.* **Happy Henry, hamburger hero**. He would open a chain of famous restaurants, called

HENRY'S! WHERE THE EATIN' CAN'T BE BEATEN!

Hmmm, well, he'd have time to
improve the name,
while collecting his
MILLIONS every
week from the
restaurant tills as
happy customers fought
their way inside for the chance to
chow down on one of **Happy Henry's**
bun-tastic burgers. Kids everywhere
would beg to eat there, safe in the
knowledge that no **vegetables** would
ever contaminate their food. Ahhh!
Horrid Henry sighed.

Mr Nudie Foodie was leaping **UP AND DOWN** with excitement. "And you're all going to help me make the delicious food that will be a joy to eat. Remember, just like the words to my hit song:

IT'S NOT RUDE
TO BE A DUDE
WHO LOVES NUDE FOOD.
YEE HAW."

"Well, Nudie," said Mrs Oddbod. "Uhh, I mean, Mr Foodie . . ."

"Just call me Mr Nudie Foodie," said **Mr Nudie Foodie**. "Now, who wants to be a nudie foodie and join me in the kitchen to make lunch today?"

"Me!" shouted Perfect Peter.

"Me!" shouted Clever Clare.

"I want to be a nudie foodie," said Jolly Josh.

"I want to be a nudie foodie," said Tidy Ted.

"I want to be a nudie foodie," yelled Greedy Graham. "I think."

"A healthy school is a happy school," said Mr Nudie Foodie, beaming. "My motto is: Only bad food boos, when you choose yummy food. And at

55

lunchtime today, all your parents will be coming to the cafeteria to sample our **scrumptious**, **YUMMALICIOUS**, **FABULICIOUS** and irresistible new food! Olé!"

Horrid Henry looked round the school kitchen. He'd never seen so many pots and pans and vats and cauldrons. So this was where the **school glop** was made. Well, not any longer. Would they be making

GIANT WHOPPER BURGERS in the huge frying pans? Or vats and vats of chips in the **HUGE** pots? Maybe they'd make pizzas for the **GIGANTIC** ovens!

The Nudie Foodie stood before Henry's class. "This is so exciting," he said, bouncing **UP AND DOWN**. "Everyone ready to make some delicious food?"

"Yes!" bellowed Henry's class.

"Right, then, let's get cooking," said Mr Nudie Foodie.

Horrid Henry stood in front of a chopping board with Weepy William,

Dizzy Dave and Fiery Fiona. Fiery
Fiona shoved Henry.

"Stop hogging the chopping board,"
she hissed.

Horrid Henry **shoved** her
back, knocking the lumpy bag of
ingredients on to the floor.

"Stop hogging it yourself," he hissed
back.

"Wah!" wailed Weepy William.
"Henry pushed me."

Wait. What was *rolling* all over the
floor? It looked like . . . it couldn't be . . .

"Group One, here's how to slice a

yummy green pepper," beamed Mr Nudie Foodie. "And Group Two, you're in charge of the **tomatoes** . . . Group Three, you make the **broccoli** salad. Group Four will look after the **MUSHROOMS**."

Green pepper? **Tomatoes?** Broccoli? **MUSHROOMS?** What was this muck?

"It's my yummy, scrummy, super, secret, vege-tastic pasta sauce!" said Mr Nudie Foodie.

WHAT? What a dirty rotten trick. Where were the chips? Where were the burgers?

59

And then
suddenly **Horrid
Henry** understood Mr
Nudie Foodie's *evil* plan. He was going
to sneak **vegetables** on to the school
menu. Not just a single vegetable,
but **LOADS AND LOADS AND LOADS** of
vegetables. Enough evil **vegetables** to
kill someone a hundred times over. Boy
impaled by **killer carrot**. Girl chokes to

death on **DEADLY BROCCOLI**. Boy gags on **TOXIC TOMATO**. Henry could see the headlines now. They'd find him **DEAD** in the lunchroom, poisoned by vegetables, his limbs twisted in agony . . .

Well, **no way**. No way was this foul fiend going to trick Henry into eating vegetables.

Everyone chopped and stirred and mixed. The evil brew **HISSED** and **bubbled**. Horrid Henry had never felt so cheated in his life.

Finally, the bell rang.

Mr Nudie Foodie stood by the exit
with an **ENORMOUS** black bin bag.

"Before you leave I want you to
open your lunchboxes and dump all
your junk food in here. No need for
that stuff today."

"Huh?" said Rude Ralph.

"No!" wailed Greedy Graham.

"Yes!" said Mr Nudie Foodie. "You'll thank me later."

Horrid Henry gasped in horror as everyone threw their **YUMMY** snacks into the bag as they filed out of the kitchen and ran out for playtime. For once Henry was glad his **MEAN**, **HORRIBLE** parents never packed anything good in *his* lunchbox.

Was there no end to this *evil* man's plots? thought Horrid Henry, stomping past **Mr Nudie Foodie** into the hall. First, vegetable pasta sauce, then

STEALING everyone's sweets? What a waste. All those treats going straight into the bin . . .

"RESCUE US, HENRY!" squealed the chocolate and crisps trapped inside the bin bag. "Help!"

Horrid Henry didn't need to be asked twice. He crept down the hall and *darted* back into the school kitchen.

Sweets, here I come, thought Horrid Henry.

The kitchen was empty. Huge vats of vegetable sauce sat ready to be poured on to pasta. What horrors would Mr Nudie Foodie try to sneak on the menu tomorrow? And the next day? And the next? Just wait until the parents discovered the sauce was made of vegetables. They'd make the children eat this swill every day. **AAAAARRRRRGGGHHHHH!**

And then suddenly **Horrid Henry** knew what he had to do. He looked longingly at the enormous black bin bag **BULGING** with crisps and chocolate and **YUMMY** snacks. Horrid Henry gritted his teeth. Sometimes you had to think ahead. Sometimes you couldn't be distracted. Not even by **DOUGHNUTS**.

There wasn't a moment to lose. Any second a teacher or dinner lady could come in and foil him. He had to seize his chance to stop **Mr Nudie Foodie** once and for all.

Grabbing whatever was nearest, **Horrid Henry** emptied a tin of salt into the first vat of sauce. Into the second went a tin of mustard powder. Into the third went a bottle of vinegar. Into the fourth and final one . . .

Henry looked at the **gurgling**, **BUBBLING**, **POISONOUS**, **reeking**, **rancid**, **TOXIC** sauce. Take

that, Nudie Foodie, thought Horrid
Henry, reaching for a tub of lard.

"What are you doing, Henry?"
rasped a deadly voice.

Henry froze.

"Just looking for my lunchbox," he
said, pretending to search behind the
cooking pots.

MISS BATTLE-AXE snarled, flashing her
yellow brick teeth. She pointed to the
door. **Horrid Henry** ran out.

Phew. What a lucky escape. Shame
he hadn't completed his mission, but
three vats out of four wasn't bad.

Anyway, the fourth pot was sure to be disgusting, even without extra dollops of lard.

You are **DEAD MEAT**, Mr Nudie Foodie, thought Horrid Henry.

"Parents, children, prepare yourselves for a **TASTE SENSATION!**" said **Mr Nudie Foodie**, ladling out pasta and sauce.

Lazy Linda's mother took a big forkful. "Hmm, doesn't this look yummy!" she said.

"It's about time this school served proper food," said Moody Margaret's mum, shovelling an **ENORMOUS** spoonful into her mouth.

"I couldn't agree more," said Tidy Ted's dad, scooping up pasta.

"BLECCCCHHHHH!" spluttered Margaret's mother, spitting it out all

over Aerobic Al's dad. Her face was purple. "That's disgusting! My Maggie Moo Moo won't be touching a drop of that!"

"**WHAT ARE YOU TRYING TO DO, POISON PEOPLE?!**" screamed Aerobic Al's dad. His face was green.

"I'm not eating this muck!" shouted Clever Clare's mum. "And Clare certainly isn't."

"But . . . but . . ." gasped Mr Nudie Foodie. "This sauce is my speciality, it's delicious, it's—" He took a mouthful.

"**UGGGHHHH**," he said, spewing it all over Mrs Oddbod. "It **IS** disgusting."

WOW, thought **Horrid Henry**. Wow. Could the sauce really be *so* bad? He had to try it. Would he get the salty, the mustardy, the vinegary, or just the plain disgusting vegetably?

Henry picked up a **TINY** forkful of pasta, put it in his mouth and swallowed.

He was still breathing. He was still alive. Everyone at his table was **slurping** up the food and beaming. Everyone at the other tables was **COUGHING** and *choking* and *SPITTING* . . .

Horrid Henry took another teeny tiny taste.

The sauce was . . . **DELICIOUS**. It was much nicer than the regular glop they served at lunchtime with pasta. It was a **MILLION BILLION** times nicer. And he had just . . . he had just . . .

"Is this some kind of joke?" gasped Mrs Oddbod, gagging. "Mr Nudie Foodie, you are toast! Leave here at once!"

Mr Nudie Foodie slunk off.

"NOOOOO!" screamed Horrid Henry. "It's yummy! Don't go!"

Everyone stared at Horrid Henry.

"Weird," said Rude Ralph.

HORRID HENRY

TELLS IT LIKE IT IS

Why, asked Horrid Henry, was he uniquely cursed?

Why, of all the homework in the world, did he have to make a five minute movie about his **GAG–BLECCCCH–YUCK** family instead of a thrilling film about **mutant zombies** or **WEREWOLF** teachers?

Ugghh. His family were **SO** boring. **Horrid Henry** yawned just thinking about them.

He was a famous film director. He'd made the soon-to-be **HOLLYWOOD** classic, *The Undead Demon Monster*

Who Would Not Die. And the sequel – *The Revenge Of The Undead Demon Monster Who Would Not Die.* Part 3 would be coming soon – *The Undead Demon Monster Who Would Not Die: This Time It's Personal!!!* He was an artist. A genius. How dare **MISS BATTLE-AXE** tell a filmmaker like him what

kind of movie to make? When he
moved to **HOLLYWOOD**, he'd have
MISS BATTLE-AXE play a **CORPSE**
in every film he made. And do all
her own stunts. Falling out of a
SKYSCRAPER. Tightrope walking between
two buildings. Being caught in an
avalanche.

AAAARRGGHH!

Why couldn't he just make the film
he wanted? He liked films about
MONSTERS. And GHOSTS.
And aliens.

But no. Their topic was All About
My Family and that's what he had
to do.

Naturally he'd left it to the last
minute.

"I need to borrow your camera,"
said Henry after a **REVOLTING**
supper of Vegetable Bake with extra
Brussels sprouts and fruit for — **ha
ha** — "dessert". "I have to ask you

questions about our family and film
you. It's homework."

He **SCOWLED**.

Mum stopped stacking dirty plates.

"When's it due?" said Mum.

Henry had hoped she wouldn't ask
that.

"Ummm . . . let me see . . . tomorrow," said Henry.

"Why do you always leave everything to the last minute?" said Dad.

Wasn't it obvious? Who wanted to do boring homework when there were so many (OMI(S to read and so much good TELLY to watch and so many packets of crisps to eat? His parents were dummies.

"I don't leave anything to the last minute," said Perfect Peter. "I always do my homework the moment I get

home from school."

Mum smiled at him. "Quite right, Peter."

"**SHUT UP**, Peter," said Henry.

"Mum, Henry told me to shut up," said Peter.

"Don't tell your brother to shut up," said Mum.

"I wouldn't have to if he wasn't so **ANNOYING**," said Henry.

"I'm not annoying, Henry's annoying," said Peter.

Horrid Henry laughed.

"Why are you laughing?" said Peter.

"I'm laughing at your **wibble wobble pants**," said Henry.

Peter looked down at his trousers.

"I don't have wibble wobble pants," said Peter.

"Do too."

"Do not."

"Do too, **Nappy Noodle Wibble Wobble Pants**."

"Mum!" screamed Peter. "Henry called me a Nappy Noodle **AND** a Wibble Wobble Pants."

"Don't be **HORRID**, Henry," shouted Mum. "Or no filming."

"But it's for homework!" shrieked Henry.

"Can we get on with this?" said Dad. "I'm very busy."

"All right," said Henry. "I'll be quick." Boy would he ever. Just a few minutes and everyone's misery — especially his — would be over.

"Do a sound check first," said

Dad. "Make sure it's loud enough and recording."

"Okay," said Henry. He pointed the camera and switched it on.

"Say **DISGUSTING. Horrible. YUCK**," said Henry.

"Disgusting. Horrible. Yuck," said Dad. Henry pressed Replay.

"**DISGUSTING. Horrible. YUCK**," came Dad's voice, loud and clear.

"This film is called ALL ABOUT MY FAMILY," said Henry, pointing the camera at Dad.

Now, what to ask, what to ask?
thought Henry.

FAT FLUFFY started snoring in
the corner.

"Dad, how would you describe our
cat FLUFFY?"

Dad paused.

"A **BIG** fatty," said Dad. "To be
honest, she really needs to lose
weight. Why does she eat so much?
Every time I see her she's chomping
away."

"Sound check, Mum," said Henry. "Smelly. **REVOLTING**. **ICK**."

"Smelly. Revolting. Ick," said Mum.

Henry pointed the camera at his mother wiping the table.

"Mum, say three adjectives that describe you," said Henry.

"Oh, uhhm, hard-working, kind, thoughtful," said Mum.

I'd say mean, bossy and grumpy, thought Horrid Henry. Too bad he wasn't answering the questions.

"Who's your favourite child, Mum?"

"Henry!" snapped Mum. "Don't be **HORRID**."

"All right," said Henry, scowling. He was only trying to make things a bit more **FUN**.

"What's your favourite **UNDEAD MONSTER?**"

"Afraid I don't have one," said Mum.

Why did he have such **boring** parents? How could someone not have a favourite undead monster? thought Henry.

"Dad, who is your eldest son?"

"Henry."

"Who is your youngest son?"

"Peter," said Mum, smiling.

"Definitely Peter," said Dad.

Henry swivelled the camera to Peter. Peter beamed and waved.

"Hello," said Peter. "Do you want to see my Bunnikins?"

"No," said Henry.

"When are you going to interview me?" said Peter. "I'm in your family."

"Worse luck," muttered Henry.

"Now, **worm**, to check the sound, can you say **WIBBLE WOBBLE POOPY PANTS?**"

"I don't want to say Wibble Wobble Poopy Pants!" screamed Peter.

"Don't be **HORRID**, Henry," said Dad. "I don't want to hear any more Wibble Wobble Poopy Pants from you."

"Okay, okay," said Horrid Henry. "Say **FANTASTIC**. Marvellous. *The best.*"

"Fantastic. Marvellous. The best," said Peter.

"What's your name?" Henry was practically falling asleep.

"Peter," said Peter.

"Who's your favourite teacher?"

"Miss Lovely."

"Tell me about your wonderful brother Henry," said Henry.

Peter paused.

"Henry is my **BIG** brother," said Peter. "He's mean to me."

"Peter!" said Mum.

"Well, he is. And I want everyone to know."

"And you're a **worm**," said Henry.

"Mum!" wailed Peter.

"What do you think about my teacher, Miss Battle-Axe?" said Henry, pointing the camera at Dad.

"She's **brilliant,**" said Dad.

"Mum!" wailed Peter again. "Henry called me a **worm.**"

"What do you think about Miss Lovely?" said Henry.

"The best teacher in the school," said Dad.

Blah blah blah. That was surely enough. **Horrid Henry** switched off the camera.

"That's . . . uhh . . . great," said Henry. **NOT.**

Horrid Henry sat on his bed and played back his film. It was even more **BORING** than he'd feared. His reputation as a *great filmmaker* would be ruined.

Wasn't there any way he could make it more interesting? More fun? More unique?

Then Horrid Henry watched the film again. And again. Hmmm. Hmmm.

What about if he . . . jiggled things around a bit? After all, wasn't editing what set a film director apart from the crowd?

95

Henry sat down at his computer and went to work. A little SNIP here, a little trim there . . .

"Right, everyone face the front," barked **MISS BATTLE-AXE**.

"Graham! Put those crisps away. Ralph! Stop **BURPING**. Meg! Stop shouting."

Graham kept eating. Ralph kept
BURPING. Megaphone Meg kept shouting.
MISS BATTLE-AXE mopped her brow.
One day she would wake up and this
would all be a BAD DREAM and
she would be doing her
real job tap dancing on
BROADWAY.

"We're going
to watch your
All About My
Family
films," she
said.

"Mine!" shrieked Megaphone Meg.

"Mine!" shrieked Fiery Fiona.

"Mine!" shrieked Zippy Zoe.

"I'll start with someone who is sitting beautifully."

Miss Battle-Axe peered round the class. The only person sitting beautifully was **MOODY MARGARET**, who was pretending she hadn't just *pulled* Sour Susan's hair when **MISS BATTLE-AXE** wasn't looking.

Miss Battle-Axe pressed **PLAY**.

There was Margaret, looking like a **HIDEOUS** frog as usual. She

was wearing
lipstick and a
BIG BOW
in her hair.

"All About My Family," said Moody
Margaret. "But naturally, this film
is about the most *interesting* and
important person in my family, me."

The camera swivelled.

"So, Mum," said Margaret,
"everyone wants to know, why am
I the most **AMAZING** person
who has ever lived in the history
of the world?"

"Ooh, *Maggie Moo Moo*," said Margaret's mum, "I'm not sure five minutes is long enough to list all your wonderful qualities."

Horrid Henry mooed under his breath.

"That's right, *Maggie Plumpykins*," said her dad. "We couldn't begin—"

"Obviously not, but hurry up and start," snapped Margaret, turning

the camera back
on herself.

"You're the most
beautiful, *talented*,
CLEVER, **AMAZING**,
brilliant, remarkable, extra—"

Rude Ralph belched.

"Don't be rude, Ralph," said Miss
Battle-Axe.

Henry made a vomiting noise.

"BLECCCCCHHHHH"

"Henry! I'm warning you."

Blah blah blah. Five long
HORRIBLE minutes of Margaret's

parents bragging about her. It felt like five years.

YΘWП. When would they get to the star of the day?

"Now, Margaret, you can choose whose film we watch next," said Miss Battle-Axe.

Sour Susan smirked.

Margaret swept her eyes over the class.

"William's," she said.

MISS BATTLE-AXE pressed **PLAY**.

There was a shot of a white ceiling. Then the film *zoomed* down to a pair of feet. There was a bit of mumbling in the background. Then the sound of weeping.

"WAH!" wailed Weepy William. He burst into tears. "I did it wrong."

Beefy Bert's film was next.

"I dunno," said Bert's mum.

"I dunno," said Bert's dad.

"I dunno," said Bert's brother.

Miss Battle-Axe frowned.

Horrid Henry waved his hand frantically.

"All right, Henry," said Miss Battle-Axe. She pressed **PLAY**.

The film opened in the kitchen. Mum, Dad and Peter were sitting smiling at the messy table.

"Dad, how would you describe Mrs Oddbod?" came Henry's voice off-camera.

"A **BIG FATTY**," said Dad. "To be honest, she really needs to lose weight. Why does she eat so much? Every time I see her she's chomping away."

"Mum, say three adjectives that describe me."

"Oh, *hard-working*, kind, **thoughtful**," said Mum, beaming.

"Mum, say three adjectives that describe Peter."

"Smelly. **REVOLTING**. **ICK**," said Mum.

"What's your favourite undead monster?"

"Peter," said Mum.

"Who's your favourite child, Mum?"

"**HENRY!**" shouted Mum.

"Who is your best son?" asked Henry.

"**HENRY**," said Dad.

"Who is the most **HORRIBLE** person you know?"

"Peter," said Mum smiling.

"Definitely Peter," said Dad.

The camera switched to Peter.

Peter smiled and waved.

"Hello," said Peter. "Do you want to see my Bunnikins?"

"No," said Henry.

"When are you going to interview me?" said Peter. "I'm in your family."

"What's your name?" came Henry's voice-over.

"**Wibble Wobble Poopy Pants**," yelled Peter.

"Who's your **WORST** teacher?"

"Miss Lovely."

"Tell me about your wonderful

107

brother Henry," said Henry.

"Henry is my big brother. He's . . . **FANTASTIC**. **MARVELLOUS**. *The best*."

"Peter!" said Mum.

"Well, he is. I want everyone to know," said Peter.

"What do you think about my teacher Miss Battle-Axe?"

"**Smelly**. **REVOLTING**. **ICK**," said Mum.

"What do you think about Miss Lovely?"

"**Wibble Wobble Poopy Pants**," said Dad.

108

"Well," said Mrs Oddbod, switching off her computer.

Mum, Dad and Henry sat in her office. Mum and Dad looked like they wished a magic carpet would fly in and *whisk* them off to a faraway planet.

"Henry, how could you?" said Mum.

"We're **SHOCKED**," said Dad.

"We're **APPALLED**," said Mum.

Horrid Henry scowled.

Honestly.

Was this the thanks he got for trying hard at homework for once?

Geniuses are never recognised in their lifetime, thought Horrid Henry sadly.

HORRID
HENRY'S
HOMEWORK

Ahhhh, thought Horrid Henry. He turned on the TV and stretched out. School was over. What could be better than lying on the sofa all afternoon, eating **CRISPS** and watching TV? Wasn't life grand?

Then Mum came in. She did not look like a mum who thought life was grand. She looked like a mum on the **WARPATH** against boys who lay on sofas all afternoon, eating crisps and watching TV.

"Get your feet off the sofa, Henry!"

said Mum.

"**unh**," grunted Henry.

"Stop getting crisps everywhere!" snapped Mum.

"**unh**," grunted Henry.

"Have you done your homework, Henry?" said Mum.

Henry didn't answer.

"**HENRY!**" shouted Mum.

"**WHAT!**" shouted Henry.

"Have you done your homework?"

"What homework?" said Henry. He kept his eyes glued to the TV.

"**GO, MUTANTS!**" he *screeched*.

"The five spelling words you are meant to learn tonight," said Mum.

"Oh," said Henry. "*That* homework."

Horrid Henry ~~HATED~~ homework. He had far better things to do with his precious time than learn how to spell "zipper" or work out the answer to 6 x 7. For weeks Henry's homework sheets had ended up in the recycling box until Dad found them. Henry swore he had no idea how they got there and blamed Fluffy the cat, but since then Mum and Dad had checked his school bag every day.

Mum snatched the zapper and switched off the telly.

"HEY, I'M WATCHING!" said Henry.

"When are you going to do your homework, Henry?" said Mum.

"SOON!" screamed Henry. He'd just returned from a long, hard day at school. Couldn't he have any peace around here? When he was king anyone who said the word **"HOMEWORK"** would get **thrown** to the crocodiles.

"I had a phone call today from Miss Battle-Axe," said Mum. "She said you got a zero in the last ten spelling tests."

"That's not **MY** fault," said Henry. "First I **lost** the words, then I **forgot**, then I couldn't **read** my writing, then I **copied** the words **wrong**, then—"

"I don't want to hear any more **SILLY** excuses," said Mum. "Do you know your spelling words for tomorrow?"

"Yes," lied Henry.

"Where's the list?" Mum asked.

"I don't know," said Henry.

"Find it or **NO TV FOR A MONTH**," said Mum.

"It's not fair," MUTTERED Henry, digging the crumpled spelling list out of his pocket.

Mum looked at it.

"There's going to be a test tomorrow," she said. "How do you spell 'GOAT'?"

"Don't you know how, Mum?" asked Henry.

"Henry . . ." said Mum.

Henry **SCOWLED**.

"I'm busy," moaned Henry. "I promise I'll tell you right after **Mutant Madman**. It's my favourite show."

"How do you spell '**GOAT**'?" said Mum.

"**G-O-T-E**," snapped Henry.

"Wrong," said Mum. "What about '**BOAT**'?"

"**WHY DO I HAVE TO DO THIS?**" wailed Henry.

"Because it's your homework," said Mum. "You have to learn how to spell."

"But **WHY?**" said Henry.

"I never write letters."

"Because," said Mum. "Now spell BOAT."

"**B-O-T-T-E**," said Henry.

"No more TV until you do your homework," said Mum.

"I've done all *my* homework," said Perfect Peter. "In fact I enjoyed it so much I've already done tomorrow's homework as well."

Henry *pounced* on Peter. He was a cannibal **tenderising** his victim for the pot.

"EEEEYOWWWW!"

screamed Peter.

"Henry! Go to your room!"

shouted Mum. "And don't come out until you know *all* your spelling words!"

Horrid Henry **STOMPED** upstairs and *slammed* his bedroom door. This was so unfair! He was far too busy to bother with **stupid**, **boring**, **useless** spelling. For instance, he hadn't read the new **Mutant Madman** comic book. He hadn't finished drawing that treasure map. And he hadn't even begun to sort his new collection of TWIZZLE cards. Homework would have to wait.

There was just one problem. Miss Battle-Axe had said that everyone who spelled all their words correctly tomorrow would get a pack of BIG BOPPER sweets. Henry LOVED Big Bopper sweets. Mum and Dad hardly ever let him have them. But why on earth did he have to learn **Spelling** words to get some? If *he* were the teacher, he'd only give sweets to

children who
couldn't spell.
Henry sighed.
He'd just have to
sit down and learn those stupid
words.

4:30. Mum **burst** into the room.
Henry was lying on his bed reading
a comic.

"**HENRY!** Why aren't you doing your
homework?" said Mum.

"I'll do it in a sec,"
said Henry. "I'm just
finishing this page."

"Henry . . ." said Mum.

Henry put down the comic.

Mum left. Henry picked up the comic.

5:30. Dad **burst** into the room. Henry was playing with his knights.

"**Henry!** Why aren't you doing your homework?" said Dad.

"**I'm tired!**" yawned Henry. "I'm just taking a LITTLE break. It's hard having so much work!"

"Henry, you've only got **FIVE** words to learn!" said Dad. "And you've just spent **TWO** hours *NOT* learning them."

"All right," **SNARLED** Henry.
Slowly, he picked up his spelling list.
Then he put it down again. He had
to get in the mood. Soothing music,
that's what he needed. Horrid Henry
switched on his cassette player. The
terrible sound of the **Driller Cannibals**
boomed through the house.

"OH, I'M A CAN-CAN-CANNIBAL!"
screamed Henry, stomping around
his room. "DON'T CALL ME AN
ANIMAL JUST 'CAUSE I'M A CAN-
CAN-CANNIBAL!"

Mum and Dad *stormed* into Henry's

125

bedroom and turned off the music.

"That's enough, Henry!" said Dad.

"DO YOUR HOMEWORK!"
screamed Mum.

**"IF YOU DON'T GET EVERY SINGLE WORD
RIGHT IN YOUR TEST TOMORROW THERE
WILL BE NO TELEVISION FOR A WEEK!"**

shouted Dad.

EEEK! No TV *and* no sweets! This was too much. Horrid Henry looked at his spelling words with loathing.

GOAT
BOAT
SAID
STOAT
FRIEND

"I hate goats! I'll never need to spell the word 'GOAT' in my life," said

Henry. He HATED goat's cheese. He HATED goat's milk. He thought goats were SMELLY. That was one word he'd definitely never need to know.

The next word was "BOAT". Who needs to spell that? thought Henry. I'm not going to be a sailor when I grow up. I get SEASICK. In fact, it's bad for my health to learn how to spell "BOAT".

As for "SAID", what did it matter if he spelt it "Sed"? It was perfectly understandable, written "Sed". Only an old fusspot like Miss Battle-Axe would mind such a TINY mistake.

Then there was "STOAT". What on earth was a stoat? What a MEAN, *sneaky* word. Henry wouldn't know a stoat if it sat on him. Of all the **USELESS**, **horrible** words, "STOAT" was the worst. Trust his teacher, **MISS BATTLE-AXE**, to make him learn a **horrible**,

USELESS word like "stoat".

The last word was **"FRIEND"**. Well, a real friend like Rude Ralph didn't care how the word **"FRIEND"** was spelt. As far as Henry was concerned any friend who minded how he spelt **"FRIEND"** was no friend. Miss Battle-Axe included that word to torture him.

FIVE WHOLE SPELLING WORDS. It was too much. I'll never learn so many words, thought Henry. But what about tomorrow? He'd have to watch Moody Margaret and Jolly Josh and

Clever Clare chomping away at those delicious BIG BOPPERS, while he, Henry, had to gnash his empty teeth. PLUS NO TV FOR A WEEK! Henry couldn't live that long without TV! He was SUNK. He was DOOMED to be sweetless, and TV-less.

But wait. What if there was a way to get those sweets without the horrid hassle of learning to spell? Suddenly, Henry had a brilliant, SPECTACULAR idea.

It was so simple Henry couldn't believe he'd never thought of it before.

He sat next to Clever Clare. Clare **always** knew the spelling words. All Henry had to do was to take a little PEEK at her work. If he positioned his chair right, he'd easily be able to see what she wrote. And he wouldn't be copying her, no way. Just double-checking. **I AM A GENIUS**, thought Horrid Henry. **100**% right on the test. Loads of BIG BOPPER sweets. Mum and Dad would be so *thrilled* they'd let him watch extra TV. **Hurray!**

Horrid Henry *swaggered* into class the next morning. He sat down in his seat between Clever Clare and Beefy Bert. Carefully, he INCHED his chair over a fraction so that he had a good view of Clare's paper.

"**SPELLING TEST!**" barked **MISS BATTLE-AXE**. "First word — GOAT."

Clare bent over her paper. Henry pretended he was staring at the wall, then, *quick as a flash*, he glanced at her work and wrote "goat".

"BOAT," said Miss Battle-Axe. Again Horrid Henry sneaked a look at Clare's paper and copied her.

AND AGAIN.

AND AGAIN.

This is FANTASTIC, thought Henry. I'll never have to learn any

spelling words. Just think of all the comic books he could read instead of wasting his time on homework! He sneaked a peek at Beefy Bert's paper. Blank. Ha ha, thought Henry.

There was only one word left.

Henry could taste the *tingly tang* of a BIG BOPPER already. Wouldn't he *swagger* about! And no way would he share his sweets with anyone.

Suddenly, Clare shifted position and edged away from him. RATS! Henry couldn't see her paper any more.

"LAST WORD," boomed Miss Battle-Axe. "**FRIEND**."

Henry twisted in his seat. He could see the first four words. He just needed to get a TINY bit closer . . .

Clare looked at him. Henry *stared* at the ceiling. Clare *glared*, then looked back at her paper. Quickly, Henry leaned over and . . . **YES!** He copied down the final word, "friend".

VICTORY!

CHOMP! CHOMP! CHOMP! Hmmnn, boy,
did those BIG BOPPERS
taste great!

Someone TAPPED him on the shoulder.
It was **MISS BATTLE-AXE**. She was
smiling at him with her **great big
yellow teeth**. Miss Battle-Axe had

never smiled at Henry before.

"Well, Henry," said Miss Battle-Axe. "What an improvement! I'm *thrilled*."

"Thank you," said Henry modestly.

"In fact, you've done so well I'm promoting you to the top spelling group. **TWENTY-FIVE EXTRA WORDS A NIGHT**. Here's the list."

Horrid Henry's jaws stopped **CHOMPING**. He looked in horror at the new spelling list. It was littered with words. But not just any words. **Awful** words. **MEAN** words. **Long** words. **HARD** words.

HIEROGLYPHS.

TRAPEZIUM.

DIARRHOEA.

"AAAAAHHHHHHHHHHH!"
shrieked Horrid Henry.

HORRID
HENRY
STEALS THE
SHOW

"How many badges do you have, Henry?" asked Perfect Peter.

"Tons," said **Horrid Henry**. "Now out of my way, worm, I'm busy." He'd just got hold of the latest **SKELETON SKUNK AND THE WIZARD OF WONDER** story and was desperately trying to finish it before Dad started **NAGGING** him to do his homework.

"I already have ten badges," said Perfect Peter. "That's five more than I need to go on the school trip to **WILD WATER-SLIDE PARK**."

"Bully for you," said Horrid Henry.

"You know that tomorrow is the deadline to earn all your badges," said Peter.

Horrid Henry stopped reading.

WHAT? **WHAT?**

That was IMPOSSIBLE.

He had weeks and weeks and weeks left to get those *stupid* badges. Hadn't he already signed up to do the sound effects for Miss Battle-Axe's dreadful school play, *THE GOOD FOOD FAIRY*, just so he could earn his Entertainer badge?

And now he had to earn **FOUR** more? **BY TOMORROW?**

144

It was so unfair.

But there was no time to lose if he wanted to race down the **ZOOM OF DOOM**, the most **TERRIFYING** water slide in the universe, or **Belly Flop Drop**, or all the other **BRILLIANT**, *amazing*, **FANTASTIC** rides at the best water-slide rollercoaster park in the **WHOLE WIDE WORLD**. Horrid Henry had always wanted to go. But his mean, **horrible** parents would never take him.

Horrid Henry pushed past Peter, dashed to his bedroom and grabbed the Badge Sheet he'd been given ages ago from under a pile of **DIRTY SOCKS** and **MUDDY JEANS**. Frantically, he skimmed it, searching for the *quickest*, **easiest** badges to earn.

Why did so many badges involve hard work? Ugh. Where was the **TV-WATCHING BADGE** when he needed it?

Horrid Henry scanned the list. Let's see, let's see — *Take Care of an Animal* badge. He took care of **FAT** Fluffy, didn't he, by letting him sleep all the time. Oh wait. *Look after an animal for two months.* Henry

didn't have two months, he had
one night.

Hiking badge? No way. Horrid
Henry **SHUDDERED**. Too dangerous.
RAMPAGING CHICKENS, **MARAUDING**
VAMPIRES — who knew what horrible
monsters were waiting just to nab
him as he *heaved* his heavy bones?

What a shame he'd been disqualified from earning the *Giving Good Advice* badge after *Vain Violet* had asked: *"How can I be more beautiful?"* and Henry had replied, **"change your head."**

Wait. Wait.

A *Cooking* badge.

YES YES YES!

"I'm cooking tonight," shouted Horrid Henry.

"I'm cooking tonight," said Perfect Peter. "I want to get another badge . . ."

Horrid Henry marched into Peter's

bedroom, grabbed Peter's favourite sheep, Fluff Puff, and DANGLED it over the loo.

"Who's cooking tonight?" said **Horrid Henry.**

"You are," wailed Peter.

Mum stared at the pile of **CRISPS** on her plate.

Dad stared at the pile of **CRISPS** on his plate.

Peter stared at the pile of **CRISPS** on his plate.

"Eat up," said Horrid Henry, stuffing **CRISPS** into his mouth. "There's seconds."

"Why are we eating **CRISPS** for dinner?" said Dad.

"It's the first course of your two-course meal so I can earn my *Cooking* badge," said Henry. "I have to include two vegetables. **OVEN CHIPS** with **Ketchup** coming up."

"This is **NOT** healthy eating," said Mum.

"Is too," said Horrid Henry. "**Ketchup** is a vegetable, which is why it's called **tomato** ketchup. **CHIPS** and **CRISPS** are made from potatoes. And I've already done the different ways to prepare and cook food part."

Hadn't he *ordered* a pizza this month? *Tick*. **Microwaved** a burger? *Tick*. And *taken the wrapper off* a chocolate bar? *Tick tick tick.* That *Cooking* badge was his.

Dad ate a handful of **CRISPS** and then patted his stomach. "I shouldn't really, I need to banish my belly," he said. "All my trousers are getting tight."

"So stop eating, **fatso**," said Horrid Henry.

"Don't be **horrid**, Henry!" said Mum.

"I'm not being **horrid**," said Henry. "I'm earning my *Handy Helper* badge by helping Dad banish his belly. So please can you sign my form? About how considerate and caring I am?"

"**NO**," said Mum.

"**NO**," said Dad.

"**ARRRRGGGGHHH!**" wailed Horrid Henry. "I need the badges **NOW**."

"You have to earn badges," said Perfect Peter.

"Quite right, Peter," said Mum.

Horrid Henry scowled. Here he was, working his **guts** off to earn badges, and his **MEAN**, **horrible** parents were being **MEAN** and **horrible.**

And as for his *wormy worm* brother . . .

"Mum, Dad, listen to the song I wrote," said Henry. "It's for my **Write and Sing a Song** badge."

Horrid Henry leapt on to a chair and started to sing.

"PETER IS A **POOP POOP POOPSICLE.**
NO ONE IS A **WORMIER WORM.**
HE'S A **NINNY** AND A **MINI**
SHOULD BE THROWN INTO A **BIN-i,**
HE'S A **POOP POOP POOP POOP POOPSICLE.**"

"Mum!" wailed Peter. "Henry called me a poopsicle."

"That's a **TERRIBLE** song, Henry," said Dad.

"No it isn't," said Henry. "It rhymes. And I wrote it myself. Where does it say it has to be a nice song?"

"Henry . . ." said Mum.

"Oh all right," said Horrid Henry.

 "I'll sing one more." If only there was a **PARENT SWAP** badge . . .

"HENRY IS THE TOP
HENRY IS THE BEST.
YOU DON'T EVEN NEED
TO PUT IT TO THE TEST.

MARGARET IS A FROG-FACE
SHE'S A DISGRACE.
I WISH SHE'D BLAST OFF

INTO OUTER SPACE –
NO! HYPER-SPACE!
THEN I'D NEVER HAVE TO SEE
THAT FROGGY FROGGY
FROG-FACE AGAIN.
RIBBIT."

Dad signed for the **Write and Sing a Song** badge.

Mum signed for the *Cooking* badge.

Dad signed for the *Handy Helper* badge but only on condition that Henry set and cleared the table for a month.

Three badges down. The fourth, the ᴇɴᴛᴇʀᴛᴀɪɴᴇʀ badge, would be his tomorrow. Then, just one more to get.

The **COLLECTOR** badge! Of course. Didn't he collect gizmos? And comics? Yes he did.

TICK.

There was one last requirement to get that badge. *Talk about someone else's collection.*

"**I hate your sheep collection, Peter!**" bellowed **Horrid Henry.**

TICK.

He'd earned the *Cooking* badge, the *Handy Helper* badge, the **Write and Sing a Song** badge and the **COLLECTOR** badge.

Just one more badge and it's **WATERPARK HERE I COME**, thought

Henry. All he had to do was the sound effects for **MISS BATTLE-AXE'S TERRIBLE** play tomorrow, and he'd be *whizzing* down the **ZOOM OF DOOM** in no time.

Horrid Henry sat backstage with the sound board on a table in front of him. All the buttons were labelled:

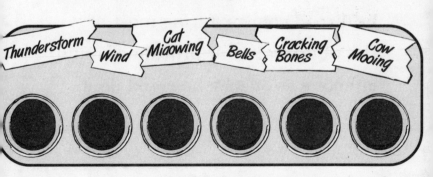

The second row sounds were:

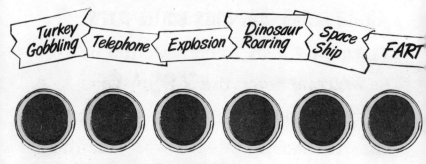

Turkey Gobbling | Telephone | Explosion | Dinosaur Roaring | Space Ship | FART

"**DO NOT TOUCH** the second row," hissed **MISS BATTLE-AXE**. "Every sound you need for this play is in the **TOP ROW**. Do exactly what we rehearsed."

Horrid Henry scowled. Naturally, he'd read comics during most of the rehearsals, but providing sound effects was *so easy* he could do it

in his sleep.

MISS BATTLE-AXE walked on to the stage.

"Welcome, everyone, to our class play, *THE GOOD FOOD FAIRY*, written by me. I'm also delighted to welcome the theatre critic from our local paper. We look forward to his review of our show."

The auditorium lights dimmed. **SOUR SUSAN** appeared, dressed in black.

"*IT WAS A DARK AND STORMY NIGHT,*" said Susan. Henry pressed the **THUNDERSTORM** button.

BANG! BANG! BANG! BOOM! BOOM! BOOM!

"**THE WIND WAS HOWLING** —" Horrid Henry pressed the *Wind* button — **Whoooooooooo** — "and snow was falling on poor, hungry Tiny Tim."

Brainy Brian sat cross-legged on stage, holding a crutch and shivering, as **ANXIOUS ANDREW** emptied a bucket of paper snow on him.

"What a **TERRIBLE** Victorian night," said Tiny Tim. "I wonder what's for supper? Wouldn't it be great to have a nice **plump** roast turkey? Oh no! **GRUEL** again! How I wish I had some fresh food like broccoli to eat. Or string beans, or tomatoes, or apples. If only I could travel to the future and enjoy a healthy meal.

"But hark! What's that I hear? It must be the *Good Food Fairy*, coming to visit."

Ding-a-ling! Ding-a-ling. Henry chimed the fairy bells as Moody Margaret swept on to the stage.

"Hello, poor person from the past," said Margaret. She waved her wand. "I've come to grant your wish. Let me show you the **wonderful** food of the future.

"First, drink *milk* and eat **cheese** for strong bones. You don't want your bones to break —"

CRUNCH CRACK
CRUNCH CRACK

"– because you haven't eaten enough calcium."

Margaret the *Good Food Fairy* continued **YAKKING** about different food groups to poor bored Tiny Tim. And the poor bored audience. "A balanced diet is made up of the five food groups," she lectured.

"1. Protein.

2. Fruit and vegetables . . ."

Horrid Henry *yawned*. He could see the theatre critic asleep in the front

row. Better wake him up, thought
Henry. After all, the storm must still
be going on.

Horrid Henry pressed the
Thunderstorm button.

**BANG BANG BANG
BOOM BOOM BOOM**

The critic woke up and *scribbled*
furiously in his notebook.

The Good Food Fairy droned on.

Horrid Henry felt his eyelids droop. What a **DULL** play. If only he, Henry, had written this play, it would have been so much more exciting. He'd have had **TERMINATOR GLADIATOR** challenge the *Good Food Fairy* to a duel for a start, then—

"Sound effect!" *hissed* Miss Battle-Axe.

YIKES, thought Horrid Henry. Which sound effect?

Horrid Henry had no idea. He *jabbed* at the sound board.

MOOOOOOOO!

The audience laughed.

OOPS. Hadn't they met the cow yet? He vaguely remembered that Tiny Tim tripped over a cow at some point.

"**I SAID,** THE GOOD FOOD FAIRY HAS LANDED ON HER DAINTY FEET," yelled Margaret, as the ear-splitting **MOOing** continued.

Horrid Henry quickly took his finger off the **Moo** button.

Dainty feet. Dainty feet? Didn't someone break a foot because they hadn't eaten enough calcium?

Horrid Henry pressed the Cracking Bones button.

CRUNCH! CRACK! CRUNCH! CRACK!

"Who's coming with us to the future?" shouted the *Good Food Fairy*, trying to be heard over the sound of breaking bones.

"Why, it's Mr Vitamin! Hello, Mr Vitamin."

Weepy William crept on to the stage.

He looked terrified.

There was a **TERRIBLE** silence.

"**SOUND EFFECT!**" *hissed* Miss Battle-Axe again.

Mr Vitamin? Who on earth was Mr Vitamin? thought Henry. Was he a **turkey**? There was a **turkey** in the play somewhere. Henry was sure someone had said **turkey**. He pressed the button.

Gobble gobble gobble, gobble gobble gobble.

"I said, 'Hello, Mr Vitamin'," repeated Margaret, glaring.

Gobble gobble gobble, gobble gobble gobble.

"MR VITAMIN," screeched Margaret. "Tiny Tim's *CAT*."

Cat? thought Henry. Boring! He should be a **DINOSAUR**. This stupid play would be so much better if he were a **DINOSAUR**.

Horrid Henry pressed the button.

ROARRRRRRRRR!

Weepy William opened his mouth
and then closed it. He'd obviously
forgotten his line.

Better help him, thought Horrid
Henry.

RING RING. RING RING.

"That's a Victorian phone," shouted
Henry from the wings. "Why don't
you answer it, Mr Vitamin?"

William didn't move.

VROOM! VROOM! VROOM! VROOM!

"Look, it's a spaceship, Mr Vitamin," shouted Henry. "Hop aboard."

"*Waaaaaaaaaaa*," wailed Weepy William.

"*I forgot my line.*"

"And now I must leave you," yelled the **Good Food Fairy**. "But before I go I must—"

A terrible fart noise blasted out.

PPPRRRRRRFFTTTTTT!

The audience howled.

Horrid Henry beamed. After all, someone had to save the show.

Horrid Henry skipped home. He'd done it! Miss Battle-Axe had refused to give him his **Entertainer** badge until she read the critic's review the next day, which ended: *"The sound effects stole the show, turning what could have been a tedious play into a comedy tour de force. I hope we see many future performances of THE GOOD FOOD FAIRY."*

Henry had no idea what a *tour de force* was, but it must have been good

because **MISS BATTLE-AXE** handed him
his Entertainer badge straight
afterwards.

"ZOOM OF DOOM, here I come!"
whooped Horrid Henry.

HORRID HENRY

CHANGES HISTORY

Blabby blabby **blabby blabby** blabby. **Blah** blah **blah** blah **blah**. History **blah**. Tudor **blah**. Henry VIII **BLAH**.

MISS BATTLE-AXE droned **oN** and **oN** and **oN**. What was she spluttering about now?

Horrid Henry lent her an ear.

Oh. She was still blabbing about that old king and his stupid wives.

Horrid Henry withdrew his ear. Back to imagining he was saving planet Earth from the intergalactic

SLIME MONSTERS by squirting them with **super-duper goo** from his super-powerful Goo-Shooter.

SPLAT! *SQUISH!* **SQUASH!**

The alien slime monster captain was covered in goo. Yes! She tried to fire back but hurrah — her laser jammed. It was filled with goo! Yes! *Superhero Heroic Henry* had done it again. He'd saved the world. All the slimy alien could do was squeak while grateful earthlings cheered and chanted his name.

"Henry! Henry! **HENRY!!!!**"

Heroic Henry looked up.

The **ALIEN SLIME MONSTER** was glaring down at him with her **bulging** red eyes and **SHARP** yellow teeth.

"I said, how many wives did King Henry VIII have?" said Miss Battle-Axe.

How was he supposed to know? thought Horrid Henry. Who knew that sort of useless fact?

"I'm waiting," said **MISS BATTLE-AXE**,

FIRE escaping from her nostrils.

"I know, I know," shouted **Moody Margaret**, waving her hand.

Must have been more than one, thought Henry. But somehow he didn't think two was the right answer.

"Nineteen?" guessed **Horrid Henry**.

"Thirty-two!" yelled Rude Ralph.

"**SIX. HE HAD SIX**," shrieked Margaret, sticking her tongue out at Henry.

"And I can name them all," said Clever Clare. "Catherine. Anne. Jane.

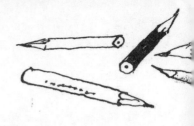

Anne. Catherine. Katherine."

"Divorced. Beheaded. Died. Divorced. Beheaded. Survived," said Miss Battle-Axe. "Well done, Clare."

Too bad that batty old **horrid Henry VIII** hadn't married **MISS BATTLE-AXE** instead of all those Catherines and Annes, thought Henry. If **MISS BATTLE-AXE** had got hold of that king, she'd have *chopped off* his head. That would have taught him to stop changing wives and boring children of the future with all those names to learn.

Anyway, who cared how many wives **KING GREEDY GUTS** had? If only Henry had been in charge, he'd have made sure Henry VIII had **NO WIVES**.

MISS BATTLE-AXE scowled at her class. One day she'd take a rocket to the moon, open a café there and eat buns all day. But until that happy moment . . .

"I have an exciting announcement," said **MISS BATTLE-AXE**. "I want everyone to write at least four pages about living in Tudor times for our class

essay competition. The competition will be judged by *Mrs Oddbod*."

Competition? Competition? A competition meant *prizes!* Horrid Henry loved prizes.

"What's the prize?" shouted Horrid Henry.

"The best prize of all — satisfaction for a job well done," said **MISS BATTLE-AXE**. "And of course, the chance to represent our school in the nationwide history quiz."

Boo. Horrid Henry **SLUMPED** in his seat.

That wasn't a prize. A prize was winning your weight in **chocolate**. Or a lifetime supply of **ice cream**. Trust birdbrain **MISS BATTLE-AXE** to think that doing a history quiz was a prize. Well, there was no danger of his winning. Horrid Henry knew almost **NOTHING** about the Tudors.

He'd **scribble** down some **RUBBISH** as fast as he could, then get back to doing something important – reading the brand-new **SCREAMIN' DEMON** comic he'd hidden under his desk.

Horrid Henry picked up his

pencil. He wasn't wasting his
valuable comic-reading time writing
four pages, that was for sure.

What a horrible thought, living in
Tudor times.

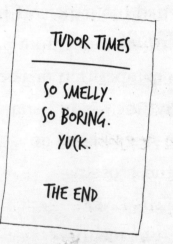

TUDOR TIMES
_____

SO SMELLY.
SO BORING.
YUCK.

THE END

Done! SCREAMIN' DEMON here I come.
Horrid Henry flung down his pencil

and opened his comic.

Oh, that Demon was playing with fire this time. Would he—

Yank! A horrible **bony** hand snatched his paper off his desk.

"**EVERYONE** must take part in the essay competition or there will be **NO** playtime today," snarled Miss Battle-Axe, GLARING at him and crossing out "THE END". "And that means writing AT LEAST four pages."

TUDOR TIMES.

SO SMELLY
SO BORING.
YUCK.

THE END

Horrid Henry gasped. No playtime? That was a **FATE WORSE THAN DEATH.**

He had no choice but to *spew* out four pages. But *why oh why* did he have to write a history essay? Why couldn't he write a story about blasting **SPACE MONSTERS?** Or fighting **SKELETON PIRATES?** Now that would be interesting.

Horrid Henry picked up his heavy pencil again. He wrote:

History. There's far too much of it. If only I'd been alive in the past to stop history, everything would be a lot better, and children would have loads more time to watch telly and eat crisps.

Take William the Conqueror. If I'd been there, I'd have ambushed William with my Goo-Shooter. He'd never have made it off the boat. He'd be William the No-Conqueror.

Then there would be **NO HISTORY** to torture students of the future. And everyone would

have lived happily ever after.

But unfortunately, I wasn't around then to save the day. Which is why we have to learn about living in Tudor times, which were **REALLY DULL.** Everyone just walked around yawning because there was nothing to do. **NO TELLY. NO COMPUTERS.** You had to wear big ruffs round your neck and prance around in **SILLY SHOES** and try not to die of boredom. Which was very hard. That's why everyone **DIED** so often.

Because there was no telly you had to go and see one of Shakespeare's long boring plays

where characters say things like "To be or not to be". Well, I say **NOT TO BE**. If I'd been there to save the day, Shakespeare would be banished to a desert island for his crimes against children of the future.

Horrid Henry put down his pencil. He was **EXHAUSTED**. He needed to write more but that was all the Tudor history he knew. He'd been fighting *INTERGALACTIC SPACE MONSTERS* while Miss Battle-Axe had been jabbering on about **TUDOR THIS** and **TUDOR THAT**.

Henry looked around. Everyone else was scribbling away while he'd barely written two pages.

Even **Beefy Bert** was writing loads.

Horrid Henry sneaked a peek at Bert's paper. Maybe he could copy him.

Bert had written:

I dunno.
I dunno.
I dunno.

Great, thought Henry. Just great.
Clever Clare was sitting in front of
him. Craning his neck, Henry could
see she was already on page eight.
If he moved his chair JUST A FRACTION to
the right, he could see a bit of Clare's
essay. Maybe he could copy her.

Sir Walter Raleigh brought back potatoes from the New World in 1587. His children were named Carew, Damerei and Walter. Queen Elizabeth I liked him very much, until she discovered that he had . . .

Henry *stretched* and **STRAINED** but he couldn't see any more.

He was on his own.

Sighing, he continued scribbling.

Walking down a smelly Tudor street, you were sure to meet Sir Walter Raleigh carrying a big sack of potatoes. He'd be with his children, who were crying because they had such weird Tudor

names: Carew and Damerei. Sir Walter was crying too, because Queen Elizabeth didn't like him any more, after she discovered he had . . .

He had what? wondered Henry. Robbed a bank? Stuck his tongue out at her? *Farted?*

. . . after she discovered he had **BAD BREATH.**

Unfortunately, you would also meet Henry VIII followed by his **SIX WIVES.** If you could, you would cross the road fast because he liked chopping off Tudor heads. You were especially

in danger if your name was **CATHERINE** or **ANNE**. Another reason why living in Tudor times was so **TERRIBLE**.

Hmmm. Well, at least he'd used the word *Tudor* loads. Did he know any other bits of history he could

stuff into his essay to make it up to four pages? Even if it wasn't about the Tudors, no one could complain it wasn't about history.

Here are a few more important history facts everyone should know.

The **BLACK DEATH** was even worse than the **PINK DEATH** or the **YELLOW DEATH**. And don't get me started on the **GREEN DEATH**. Like I said, there was lots of death in history. Which is another reason why **HISTORY IS HORRIBLE**.

Before the Tudors, there were cavemen.

They had their own kings, like **KING CLUBHEAD** and **KING STONEFACE**. They liked fighting dinosaurs, which is why dinosaurs are extinct, otherwise that **horrid King Henry VIII** would have hunted them. Come to think of it, a **T. REX** would have hunted him for a tasty snack.

Hurrah. He'd managed to write nearly four pages. A few more sentences and he'd be done.

SCREAMIN' DEMON comic here I come, thought Horrid Henry as he filled up the final page with the **biggest** handwriting he could.

It's much better to be alive today than in Tudor times. Or in the bad old olden days when history was starting.

THE END

"Time's up," said **MISS BATTLE-AXE**, collecting the papers.

That was the *perfect* essay, thought **Horrid Henry**. No way he'd win, but no one could say he hadn't tried. He opened his comic and sighed happily. Just a few more minutes till playtime.

The next morning the head, *Mrs Oddbod*, came into the classroom, holding a thick folder. She whispered to Miss Battle-Axe. **MISS BATTLE-AXE** went green.

"What do you mean, I gave out the **WRONG** topic?" she spluttered. "They weren't meant to write about the Tudors?"

"That's for next year," said *Mrs Oddbod*. "They were supposed to write about *Great Moments in History*."

MISS BATTLE-AXE sat down and wiped her brow. In thirty-five years of teaching she had never made a mistake. Maybe it was time to think about running away and joining an expedition to the South Pole.

Mrs Oddbod stood in front of
the class.

"The bad news is that you were
accidentally given the **WRONG TOPIC** for
the essay competition."

Clever Clare burst into tears. *Brainy*
Brian looked faint.

"The *good* news, however, is that one person seems to have written partly about the right topic. A very . . . ERRR . . . interesting response.

"So I am pleased to tell you that our school will be represented at the nationwide history quiz by . . . Henry."

WHAT?

HUH?

"Congratulations, Henry. We will start our history quiz preparations immediately. See me every day after school for extra practice."

Mrs Oddbod dumped a load of books on his desk.

BIG BOOKS.

fat books.

Dusty books.

what? what?

"NOOOOOOOOOOOOOOOOOO!"

HORRID
HENRY
SCHOOL STINKS!

Turn the page for
some super
fun games and
activities!

school Crossword

CAN YOU FIGURE OUT ALL THE HIDDEN WORDS IN THIS HORRID CROSSWORD PUZZLE?

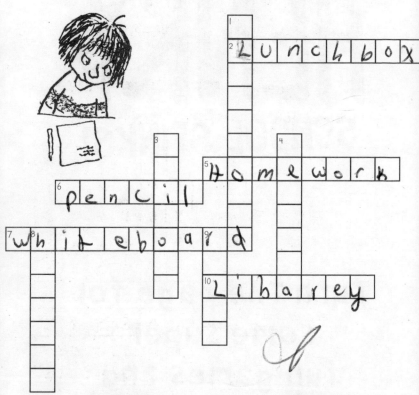

ACROSS

2. A CONTAINER FOR YOUR PACKED LUNCH
5. SCHOOL WORK YOU DO AT HOME
6. YOU USE THIS TO WRITE AND DRAW
7. YOU CAN WIPE YOUR ANSWERS OFF THIS
10. A ROOM FULL OF BOOKS

DOWN

1. WHEN IT'S BREAK TIME YOU PLAY OUT HERE
3. IN MOST SCHOOLS YOU HAVE TO WEAR A SCHOOL ...
4. THE PERSON WHO TEACHES YOU IS CALLED A ...
8. A SCHOOL SUBJECT ABOUT THE PAST
9. YOU NEED THIS TO DRAW A STRAIGHT LINE

Weepy William's Wordsearch

WEEPY WILLIAM IS STRUGGLING TO FIND ALL THE WORDS
IN THIS WORDSEARCH. CAN YOU HELP HIM?

JOLLY   GORGEOUS   WEEPY   MOODY   CLEVER

HORRID   BOSSY   PERFECT   BRAINY   RUDE

Y	P	G	Y	C	L	E	V	E	R	D	R	I	H
G	O	R	E	G	O	S	R	O	Y	M	T	E	I
V	Y	O	Y	D	Y	N	R	Y	E	Y	O	D	E
G	G	O	R	G	E	O	U	S	L	V	N	A	G
U	D	U	R	E	B	W	E	S	L	R	O	S	O
D	R	O	J	E	D	Y	J	F	E	O	C	O	Y
W	P	E	O	P	I	U	D	B	O	S	S	Y	E
Y	R	D	L	E	Y	P	R	D	H	O	H	O	H
E	N	E	L	E	V	E	N	S	D	W	O	O	O
I	O	I	Y	D	E	R	P	M	O	O	D	Y	W
E	U	O	A	O	R	F	R	L	W	E	E	P	Y
E	R	E	E	R	O	E	D	D	I	R	R	O	H
R	Y	D	R	D	B	C	Y	R	L	C	C	R	Y
A	O	O	P	T	H	T	J	Y	D	R	S	P	F

Super Sudoku

CLEVER CLAIRE LOVES DOING SUDOKUS. FILL IN NUMBERS ONE TO SIX IN THE PUZZLE. EACH NUMBER CAN ONLY APPEAR ONCE IN EACH COLUMN, ROW AND SQUARE.

1	2	3	4	5	6
4	4	5	3	1	2
2	6	1	5	4	3
5	3	4	2	6	1
6	4	2	1	3	5
3	1	5	6	2	4

NOW FOR AN EVEN HARDER ONE!

3	2	2	1	4	6	8	5	9
8	1	6	5	4	7	4	2	3
9	5	4	3	8	2	7	1	6
	8	3	2	1	9	6	4	7
					4		9	5
						3	8	
6	4	8	9	5	3		7	2
				7	1		6	8
	7	9		2				4

Miss Battle-Axe's Fun Facts

MISS BATTLE-AXE HAS SET THE CLASS SOME TRICKY TRIVIA QUESTIONS. WHY NOT CHALLENGE A FRIEND?

1. HOW MANY TEETH DOES AN ADULT HUMAN HAVE?

   32

2. WHAT IS THE WORLD'S LARGEST OCEAN?

   The Pacific Ocean

3. HOW MANY BREATHS DOES THE AVERAGE HUMAN TAKE IN A DAY?

   20,000

4. WHAT AMPHIBIAN NEVER SLEEPS?

   The bullfrog

5. HOW MANY BONES DOES A SHARK HAVE?

   Zero!

6. WHICH SLIMY CREATURE HAS FOUR NOSES?

   A slug!

Perfect Peter's Word Game

PERFECT PETER LOVES TO PLAY WITH WORDS. IN THIS GAME YOU HAVE TO CHANGE ONE LETTER OF THE WORD WITH EACH NEW LINE. THE AIM IS TO TRANSFORM THE FIRST WORD INTO THE LAST WORD.

EXAMPLE:

BOAT
COAT
CHAT
THAT
THAN

NOW YOU TRY!

1. BALL
    ___
    ___
    MEAT

2. FACE
    ___
    ___
    PORT

Moody Margaret's Marvellous Jokes

MOODY MARGARET HAS SOME NEW JOKES TO TRY OUT.
WHICH ONE DO YOU THINK IS FUNNIEST?

1. WHAT'S THE WORLD'S TALLEST BUILDING?

A library, as it has the most stories

2. WHY DO MATHS BOOKS ALWAYS LOOK SO SAD?

Because they're full of problems

3. WHAT DID THE SPIDER MAKE ONLINE?

A website

4. WHY DO CALCULATORS MAKE SUCH GREAT FRIENDS?

You can always count on them!

5. WHAT DID YOU LEARN IN SCHOOL TODAY?

Not enough, I have to go back again tomorrow!

AND NOW FOR SOME BRAIN TEASERS!

1. IT'S AS LIGHT AS A FEATHER, BUT THE STRONGEST PERSON CAN'T HOLD IT FOR MORE THAN FIVE MINUTES. WHAT IS IT?

2. WHAT GETS WETTER WHILE IT DRIES?

3. WHAT STARTS WITH A P, ENDS WITH AN E AND HAS A THOUSAND LETTERS?

4. WHAT BELONGS TO YOU BUT OTHER PEOPLE USE IT MORE THAN YOU?

5. WHAT COMES ONCE IN A MINUTE, TWICE IN A MOMENT, BUT NEVER IN A THOUSAND YEARS?

Hurry, Horrid Henry!

HELP HORRID HENRY GET TO THE
ICE CREAM IN THE MIDDLE OF THE
MAZE BEFORE IT MELTS!

START

Lights, camera, Action!

HENRY IS SHOOTING HIS OWN MOVIE, BUT THERE'S
SOMETHING WRONG WITH HIS EQUIPMENT.
CAN YOU FIND THE SIX CHANGES IN THE IMAGE
ON THE RIGHT?

How to Draw
Horrid Henry!

LEARN TO DRAW HORRID HENRY WITH THESE FIVE EASY
STEPS. GET A BLANK PIECE OF PAPER AND A PENCIL
AND FOLLOW ALONG.

1. Let's start with Henry's head. Draw a circle with two wide eyes, a curved nose and a smile.

2. Now add his messy mop of hair.

3. From the bottom of his chin draw two arms going out in opposite directions with five fingers at each end.

4. Now draw the rest of his top and add thick stripes.

5. Finally, draw two straight legs with shoes at the end. See if you can copy the picture and draw him jumping!

Don't forget to colour him in!

School Trip Search and Find!

HENRY'S CLASS ARE ON A SCHOOL TRIP TO A MUSEUM, BUT THEY'RE NOT BEHAVING WELL! CAN YOU SPOT THE THINGS IN THE LIST BELOW?

A T-REX SKELETON

HORRID HENRY

A WALRUS

A VACUUM CLEANER

AN OWL

A FOOTBALL

A WIZARD

A BAT

MISS BATTLE-AXE

A SHEEP

ANSWERS

school crossword

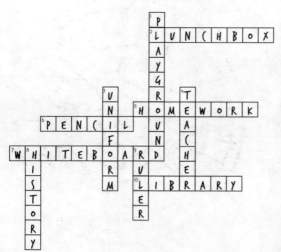

1. P
2. LUNCHBOX (L,A,Y,G,R,O,U,N,D)
3. UNIFORM
4. T
5. HOMEWORK
6. PENCIL
7. WHITEBOARD
8. HISTORY
9. RULER
10. LIBRARY
4. TEACHER

Super Sudoku

1	2	3	4	5	6
4	5	6	3	1	2
2	6	1	5	4	3
5	3	4	2	6	1
6	4	2	1	3	5
3	1	5	6	2	4

3	2	7	1	4	6	8	5	9
8	1	6	5	9	7	4	2	3
9	5	4	3	8	2	7	1	6
5	8	3	2	1	9	6	4	7
7	6	1	8	3	4	2	9	5
4	9	2	7	6	5	3	8	1
6	4	8	9	5	3	1	7	2
2	3	5	4	7	1	9	6	8
1	7	9	6	2	8	5	3	4

Weepy William's WordSearch

Y	P	G	Y	C	L	E	V	E	R	D	R	I	H
G	O	R	E	G	O	S	R	O	Y	M	T	E	I
V	Y	O	Y	D	Y	N	R	Y	E	Y	O	D	E
G	G	O	R	G	E	O	U	S	L	V	N	A	G
U	D	U	R	E	B	W	E	S	L	R	O	S	O
D	R	O	J	E	B	Y	J	F	E	O	C	O	Y
W	P	E	O	P	I	U	D	B	O	S	S	Y	E
K	R	D	L	E	Y	P	R	D	H	O	H	O	H
E	N	E	L	E	V	E	N	S	D	W	O	O	O
I	O	I	Y	D	E	R	P	M	O	O	D	Y	W
E	U	O	A	O	R	I	R	L	W	E	E	P	Y
E	R	E	E	R	O	E	D	B	I	R	R	O	H
R	Y	D	R	D	B	C	Y	R	L	C	C	R	Y
A	O	O	P	T	H	T	J	Y	D	R	S	P	F

Moody Margaret's Brain Teasers

1. YOUR BREATH
2. A TOWEL
3. POST OFFICE
4. YOUR NAME
5. THE LETTER 'M'

Perfect Peter's Word Game

1. BALL
   BELL
   BELT
   MELT
   MEAT

2. FACE
   FACT
   FART
   PART
   PORT

Hurry, Horrid Henry!

START

Lights, camera, Action!

School Trip Search and Find!

COLLECT ALL THE
HORRID HENRY STORYBOOKS!